Salvador's COUGAR

GEORGE SOLANO

ISBN 979-8-89428-429-3 (paperback)
ISBN 979-8-89428-431-6 (digital)

Christian Faith Publishing
832 Park Avenue
Meadville, PA 16335
www.christianfaithpublishing.com

Printed in the United States of America

*In memory of my mother, Adelina Solano y (and) Montoya
When I was a child, she told me that one of my
grandmothers was a full-blooded Indian*

*Also to my wife, Iona
She is my puma*

Acknowledgments

My thanks to the following websites, whose assistance was most helpful with the Comanche language, which is disappearing. Out of a population of about twelve thousand, fewer than nine hundred are fluent speakers, most of whom are elderly and are not being replaced by younger descendants.

1. http://www.comanchelanguage.org (Barbara Goodin)
2. http://www.niwic.net/hello-oklahoma (Benjamin Bruce)
3. http://digital.library.okstate.edu/chronicals
4. http://www.museumgreatplains.org/lawtoncentennial

My thanks to the following websites for the information they contain about the Santa Fe Trail.

1. http://www.newmexico.org
2. http://www.nps.gov/safe/
3. http://www.sangres.com/places/nm

Chapter 1

The White Calf

The buffalo were on the move through the low grass plains, sensing the hunters nearby. Yet they stopped and encircled the buffalo cow that was starting to give birth to her calf.

The world seemed to stand still as she continued her labor, while the prairie hens and prairie dogs, standing on their burrows, looked on in amazement. Once the calf was born, landing on the grass with a thud, the herd opened ranks and began its steady march westward.

The cow began to lick her calf and coax it to its feet so that it could suckle and gain strength before they joined the herd. They needed to move quickly before the breeze could notify the coyotes in the area of a new and helpless life.

As the herd steadily moved further westward on its trek across the southwestern plains of what would become the Colorado Territory, the cow grew restless. All her prodding and coaxing seemed to be in vain; her calf, though alive, would not stand. Had its legs been broken when it hit the ground so hard, or had it already lost the will to live?

The cow, now more restless than ever, began to nudge the calf with her nose repeatedly. She gave out a bellow, as if asking for help or requesting the herd to wait. By now, they were a good half mile away on their westward trek, yet the calf did not attempt to get up. She knew that if she did not hurry and catch up with the herd, she would either be lost and on her own or succumb to the coyotes as well.

The sun began to set in the west, and the sky filled with clouds resembling fish scales on the horizon. She prodded her calf again and again. Fearing the worst, she began to walk toward the herd. When she was fifty yards away, she looked back at her calf. When she was seventy-five yards away, her calf cried out to her. Her motherly instincts prevailed, and she returned to her calf, which still lay on the ground.

Dusk was falling, and in the distance, you could hear the coyotes as the sun hid behind the mountains.

Chapter 2

Smoke Galore

"As much as we would like to see the little white buffalo get up on its feet, we need to hurry and make camp before it is too dark," Salvador Montoya told his companions, who were standing in the arroyo along with him, all enthralled by the life-and-death struggle before them.

Each parted in their own direction, as if assignments had been made earlier. Andres Lucero began to gather all their bedrolls, then selected and prepared an area for them to sleep under the stars, as there would not be a rainstorm tonight. The sky indicated that it would rain within two days. Antonio Solano prepared an area to corral the horses and mules and took the feed for the animals out of the covered wagon, while Tomas Salazar unhitched the mules and unsaddled the horses.

Juan Trujillo had been busy gathering wood and started the fire as Salvador pulled the black kettle containing the stew he had prepared that morning. It was supposed to be their lunch, but in their haste to get to the arroyo before dark, they had not stopped for lunch. Now it would be even more savory, filled with chunks of beef, potatoes, carrots, dried peas, and corn.

They ate until the kettle was empty. As they sat around the fire drinking their coffee, Salvador mentioned that the fire had been hot and smokeless.

Tomas said, "Remember year before last when—"

"What happened?" Andres asked, for this was the first time he had come hunting. The others had been coming every year in July for six years now.

Juan, having refilled his cup of coffee, sat down and said, "Let me tell you what happened because I was responsible for what happened.

"We had arrived here early that day and had made camp before dusk. We had already eaten supper when a horde of mosquitoes descended upon us with the intent of sucking us dry. Just like when we boil the pinecones of the piñon tree to have them open so we can get at the nuts, we put some dried cow chips in the fire to keep the mosquitoes away. I got some dried buffalo chips and put them in the fire. The smoke chased away the mosquitoes, but then Jose Castellano, who was preparing to unhitch the team from the covered wagon, alerted us that a large column of dust was to the east of us and coming this way. We got rid of the horde of mosquitoes, only to bring upon us a more deadly horde.

"Instinctively, we began to saddle our horses as Jose jumped up in the driver's seat of the covered wagon and got it out of the arroyo, heading west as fast as the horses could go. The mules, still hitched to the other two wagons, took off behind the covered wagon on their own. Our horses saddled, we took off, leaving the smoking fire. Up over the arroyo, urging our mounts to give us all the speed they could muster, the mules were a good quarter of a mile behind the covered wagon. It seemed like an hour before we caught up with them and continued on our way to catch up with Jose. The Kotsoteka's, one of the known thirty-five bands of Comanches, their name meaning 'buffalo-eating people,' were still coming toward us, but they were still a good half mile behind the mules.

"Our horses, carrying us as fast as they could, started to gain on the covered wagon. Looking back at the mules about a quarter mile behind us, we continued to follow. We were now about a quarter mile behind Jose. As we gained ground on the covered wagon, the Kotsoteka's gained ground on the mules. Finally, as we reached the back of the covered wagon, we looked back and saw that the Kotsoteka's had brought the mules and the cargo in the wagons to a halt. Still, we continued at full speed for another twenty minutes. As the sun set behind the mountains, looking back, gracias a Dios [thanks be to *God*] that the Kotsoteka's had been more interested in our supplies and not our scalps. Our mounts all lathered up, we slowed to a walk to allow them to cool down. We continued to ride, changing our course more northwest before we stopped to take care of the horses."

Juan got up, went to the campfire, picked up the big blue-and-white-speckled metal coffeepot, and began to refill everyone's coffee cups, which were of the same color.

Having taken the last of the coffee for himself, Tomas, the self-proclaimed historian of the group, began to tell Andres that they had been really fortunate because the Kotsoteka Comanche were the finest horsemen of all the Indian tribes. Their ancestors had stolen their mustangs from the first few Spanish Conquistador expeditions to this region. At first, the Indians would steal the horses for meat, but once they began to ride and use the horse to pull their belongings instead of dogs, they realized that they could now have larger teepees and were able to cover thirty to forty miles per day as they followed the buffalo. The horse changed everything for them; now they could chase and kill the buffalo easier.

Salvador held out his hand toward Juan to get the empty coffeepot. As Juan sat down, Salvador finished washing the dinner plates and coffeepot and began to get things prepared for the next day.

Chapter 3

Angelita

Andres, looking at Juan, asked, "Well, what did you lose, and what happened?"

Juan began, "We lost the two mule teams and the two wagons, Tomas and I both lost our buffalo guns, and we all lost the extra change of clothes and all the extra food, water, and salt. The next day, we fed the horses and gave them what little water we had left as we continued our way to Bentt's Fort, which was located on the north shore of the Arkansas River—a rectangular fortress and trading post with fourteen-to-sixteen-foot-tall adobe walls. Once we crossed the Arkansas River, we arrived there late that afternoon. We bought what we needed to replace what we had lost and made plans to return to Mexico."

The noise of the coyotes nearby, devouring something, brought everyone's attention back to the little white buffalo. They knew the rule of survival: kill or be killed. Yet each hoped in their heart that it was something other than the white buffalo calf that the coyotes were devouring.

Brought back to reality, they chose the order in which they would keep watch. Salvador would take the first watch. As they bedded down for the night, Salvador gathered their cups, washed and dried them, and then sat down by the fire with the remainder of his lukewarm coffee.

Sitting in front of the fire, sipping the rest of his coffee, the night became silent as the others drifted off to sleep. He began to remember the last time he had been at Bent's Fort, where he had purchased all the necessary staples, three peach trees, and three yards of yellow fabric. He had wanted to buy the morning glory plant just outside the mercantile, but William Bent would not sell it, no matter how much he offered. Finally, William went out with him, showed him what the seeds looked like, and let him pick as many as he wanted.

His wife, Angelita, who was Juan Trujillo's younger sister, had been so happy when he got home that year. When she unwrapped the package containing the fabric, she lit up like the sun, clutching it to her chest as she danced around and around.

"I will make a dress out of this," she said. "On Sunday, I will be the envy of all the other women, for I want them to see how wonderful you are to me."

He sat there enjoying the moment as he watched her prance around, holding the fabric to her chest, her face radiating happiness. He so enjoyed those moments, for he would do anything for his Angelita (little angel).

He could not remember a day without his Angelita, for they had been childhood sweethearts and married when he was seventeen and she was sixteen. A year and a half into their marriage, he had almost lost her when she gave birth to their son, Marcelino, whom he had left with his brother Gregorio and his wife. A year after Marcelino's birth, Angelita complained of severe stomach pain, followed by vomiting, and for three weeks, she was in anguish. He remembered how her mother, Maria, and her younger sister, Clara, would come each day to help take care of her. He would ride for two hours to the chapel, where he paid Padre (Father) Sanchez to say Mass for her each day. He went into the chapel and knelt before the big crucifix at the altar.

There he began to pray: "God, you know me. I am Salvador, a simple man of no value, and I know I am not worthy to ask anything of you. But the padre says that if we ask for anything in the name of your Son, Jesus, you will give it to us. Well, I do not ask for anything for me, but I ask in your Son's name to heal my wife. If you need someone in her place, take me. I thank you for hearing me." With that said, he made the sign of the cross and left the chapel, heading back to his Angelita, trusting that God would make her well.

The memories continued to flood his mind, even the one he wished he could erase. It had been in June last year that the Kotsoteka band of Comanches had raided his farm. The memory flowed through his mind as if in slow motion, prolonging the pain of reliving each moment that had shattered his heart into a million pieces.

He could see himself two hundred yards east of their adobe house, at the end of the second earthen dam, replenishing the water consumed by his herd of cattle. He could see his Angelita working in the garden at the west end of the first earthen dam, kept full by the stream of water that came out of the hill on its south side. About fifty feet north of the garden and a quarter of the distance of the first earthen dam was the big corral with nineteen heads of horses in it.

Halfway on the north side of the first earthen dam was a tall weeping willow tree. Down from it, in line with the corral, was a very tall cottonwood tree. Next in line from the cottonwood tree toward the adobe house was the chicken coop and rabbit hutch. Centered twenty feet on either side from the rabbit hutch and the house stood another giant cottonwood tree. Of all the animals, his golden palomino was tethered at the back door of the house, for his father had given him that horse as a colt on his wedding day.

He could hear himself screaming, "Comanche! Comanche!" in hopes that Angelita could hear him. The Comanches were coming from the west, and it must have been a band of about twenty heading straight for Angelita and the corral. As he dropped his shovel and began to run to the house, he could see Angelita already past the weeping willow tree, running toward the house. Everything before his eyes was moving so swiftly, yet even though he was running as fast as he could, he seemed to be moving in slow motion. Two Comanches were now closing in on either side of his Angelita, the horses raising a cloud of dust as they overtook her. He was now about one hundred yards away as the two Comanches took his golden palomino and rounded the house on their way to join the rest of the band that had taken all the head of horses out of the corral. As fast as the Comanches had arrived, they were now gone.

What seemed an eternity to Salvador, he finally reached the back door of the house, running in through the dust, hoping against hope that Angelita had made it inside. Through the rooms he ran looking for Marcelino and Angelita. He found Marcelino asleep in his bed. He finished checking the rest of the rooms to no avail. Out the back door he ran, looking up toward the corral. There, about twenty feet from the giant cottonwood tree, lay Angelita, face down in the dirt.

"Angelita! Angelita!" he hollered as he ran to her. An arrow had entered her back, and as he rolled her over and cradled her in his arms, he could see the arrowhead protruding about four inches out of the center of her chest.

"Angelita! Angelita!" he cried, a drop of blood now sliding down the left corner of her mouth as her eyes opened.

"Te amo, mi querido. Cuida a Marcelino y dile que lo amo." (I love you, my darling. Take care of Marcelino and tell him that I love him.)

Tears cascaded down Salvador's cheeks as Angelita looked into his eyes, saying, "Me voy con Dios." (I go with God.) With that, she took her last breath and died in his arms.

Salvador continued to sit there, cradling her in his arms, crying and calling her name. His heart, once filled to overflowing with love, was now shattered into a million pieces. The void that held his heart was now filled with anger and hatred for the Kotsoteka Comanches.

The following morning, the Trujillos and Castellanos came by on their way to Mass, as they did every fourth Sunday. They found Salvador still sitting on the ground, cradling Angelita and crying.

Jose Castellano sent his son Jorge to the chapel to notify the padre. Then he pried Angelita from Salvador's arms and handed her to Juan. Juan, with his eyes watering, broke the arrow at the quiver and finished pulling it out the front, then gently picked up his sister and carried her into the house, laying her in the bed.

Juan composed himself as he walked back outside and went to help Jose try to console Salvador. Meanwhile, the women inside prepared Angelita for burial as they prayed the rosary.

Jorge and Padre Sanchez arrived along with the rest of the neighbors. The padre went inside, performed the last rites, and, having finished his prayers over Angelita and commending her into God's hands, went outside to talk with Salvador.

"Why did God allow this to happen?" asked Salvador. Though the padre spoke many words, Salvador did not hear them. Then, interrupting the Padre, Salvador said, "Padre, I cannot have her buried at the chapel, for I cannot be that far away from my Angelita. Please consecrate the ground under the weeping willow tree because she always sat there in the shade each evening, listening to the stream ripple into the dam."

The padre held funeral Mass there that Sunday, and Angelita was buried to the right and under the shade of the weeping willow tree.

Salvador could see himself in his mind, how each night, before going to bed, he would hold her yellow dress to his chest and smell her scent until he could no longer smell it, then leave it in the dresser drawer.

Chapter 4

The Hunt

A hand landed on Salvador's left shoulder while tears streamed down his cheeks, startling him as Andres came to relieve him and take over the watch.

*****

Tomas was still watching when Salvador awoke about two hours before dawn, as was his habit.

"Go ahead and get some more sleep," he told Tomas, "because I will be getting everything ready for breakfast."

Tomas headed back to his bedroll as Salvador began to get everything ready. Salvador added more wood to the fire, then began to take out the wrought-iron skillets, the big blue-and-white-enamel coffeepot, plates, and cups. He filled the coffeepot with water and took out the piece of cheesecloth that he always used for the coffee grounds. He smoothed it out, placed the coffee grounds in it, tied it up, and put it in the coffeepot. Even though most people just put the coffee grounds directly into the coffeepot and poured cold water over the pot to make the grounds settle to the bottom once the coffee was done, Salvador did not like grounds in his coffee. This was his way to ensure he could enjoy the last drop. He placed the coffeepot on the hook over the center of the fire, then placed one of the big wrought-iron skillets upside down on a couple of rocks that were in the fire and the rocks that encircled the fire. The bottom of this wrought-iron skillet had never seen fire, for it was used only when he was camping and only used to make his tortillas, a round unleavened bread.

The night sky was retreating, and the grayish-blue sky revealed some clouds as the horizon to the east became a pale blue. When the coffee began to boil over into the fire, Salvador grabbed the coffeepot and put it to the side until it stopped spilling over, then placed it on some of the rocks that encircled the fire. The red chili was ready, and the potatoes were almost done as Salvador began to fry the bacon and eggs in the large skillet.

The smell of the coffee had awakened the others. They had already fed and watered the horses and were now enjoying their first cup of coffee, just waiting for the eggs and bacon to fry. Half of the sun was now visible above the horizon as they sat around the fire eating breakfast. They finished eating and poured themselves another cup of coffee when Salvador said, "I am going to see what the coyotes ate last night."

They all joined Salvador and walked side by side with their coffee cups in one hand, heading to where the white buffalo had been. A smile broke out on each of their faces as there was no evidence of the white buffalo at all, giving each more hope that the little calf had gotten up and hopefully had joined the herd. They turned around and headed back to the arroyo to clean up the breakfast dishes and have some more coffee.

The arroyo they were in was about four feet deep in areas. It had been an above-ground stream, but now the water traveled about ten feet underground, then emerged and plunged an additional fifteen feet into the gorge about five miles to the east. From there, it flowed for about half a mile due east before taking a southeasterly turn, flowing into the beaver pond. From there, it continued to meander on its way southeasterly. On either side of the waterfall, where the water emerged and all the way down to the beaver pond, red-and-black raspberry bushes lined the stream.

"How far are we going to have to travel today to get the buffalo?" asked Andres.

"Not far at all," Tomas answered, "because they will be coming back to the beaver pond sometime today, and then we will get enough for everyone back home. So let's start getting things ready."

Juan and Salvador began doing the breakfast dishes and putting them away. Then they sharpened the knives they would use to skin and butcher the buffalo, placed the barrels of salt where they would be handy, and strung lines for the jerky.

As Tomas and Andres set up the tripods they would use to hang and butcher the buffalo, Tomas told Andres about how the Indian pinto had derived from the Spanish mustang and how the medicine-hat, or war-bonnet, pinto was their most prized possession, making the Comanches invincible on their raids of the Spanish settlements.

"You know, Tomas," Andres said, "I have heard it said that these Kotsoteka Comanches brag that they only allow the Spanish to remain in their region to raise horses for them. That doesn't make sense because if it were true, they would not kill any Spaniard on their raids."

Tomas had no reply to this.

All preparations were made, and they could hear and see the buffalo coming back to the beaver pond. They retrieved their buffalo guns, hoping to get at least twenty to twenty-five buffalo to supplement everyone's ration of meats in the community for the coming winter. During this time of year, the Comanche made camp about three miles east of the beaver dam along the spring, and they were confident that the buffalo guns would not be heard at that distance and over the thunder the buffalo herd would make after the first shot, causing them to start stampeding.

The buffalo herd came within the distance of the buffalo guns, and they began shooting. One buffalo down, and the herd began to stampede as they continued to shoot until the entire herd had passed. They took their horses and began to drag the buffalo to the arroyo to butcher them. Once they had them all in the arroyo, they counted nineteen. That would keep them busy for the rest of the day, butchering, skinning, preparing the hides, salting the meat, and making some jerky. Just like a well-oiled machine, they went to work, each one doing a specific job.

Thunderstorm clouds began to come over the mountains in the west. The sun was overhead and about three-quarters of the way in the sky on its way to the western horizon when they finished preparing the last buffalo they had killed. Salvador had put coffee on earlier, and now they had a chance to sit and sip a cup of coffee as they relaxed.

"All we need is seven or eight more," Antonio said, "and if we get them this evening, we can be on our way back home tomorrow. That will make this the fastest we have gotten what we needed."

They all filled their cups with coffee again as Salvador cooked some potatoes, chili, and, of course, buffalo steaks.

*****

Dishes had been washed, dried, and put away before dusk. True to nature, the buffalo were again on their westerly move. They grabbed their guns and got ready as the buffalo came within the distance of their guns. One went down, then two, three, four, five, when all at once, Antonio began to raise and lower his weapon, pointing to the rear of the herd. They all just stood there, watching the buffalo cow with her white calf keeping up with the herd. The herd now gone, they once again went out, gathered the five buffalo they had killed, and set about their task of getting them prepared. Tired out, they went to bed early that night as the clouds continued to build.

Salvador awoke at his normal time and began to prepare breakfast and get the coffee ready. When the sun began to come up over the horizon, he could see that the sky was completely overcast and gray. He woke the others; they ate breakfast, had their coffee, and began to feed and water the horses and start preparing for their departure.

Chapter 5

Cougar by the Tail

Salvador saddled his horse and put the four empty water barrels, two on each side, on one of the mules. Saddled and with the mule's bridle in his left hand, he told the others to continue making preparations for departure. "As soon as I am back, we will leave," he said, hoping they could make twenty or thirty miles before the rain started. He rode off with the mule down the arroyo to fill the barrels where the water emerged and plunged into the gorge.

Salvador arrived at the edge of the arroyo and surveyed the area below, making sure that no one was around because he did not want to run into any Comanches this morning. Everything appeared to be okay, as the only thing he noticed was a young grizzly bear at the edge of the bushes about two hundred yards downstream from where he was going to get the water. It appeared that the grizzly had been gnawing on the rib cage of what might have been a fawn. Keeping an eye on the grizzly, he began to go down into the gorge on the south side of the stream. As he descended, it appeared that the grizzly looked up and began to lumber further downstream. With each step the horse and mule made, his eyes scanned in every direction.

Arriving at the bottom and near the waterfall, he began to unlash the barrels from the mule. Once he had them all unlashed, he placed the first barrel under the waterfall to be filled.

As the last barrel was being filled, he heard the rustling of the raspberry bushes and hid in them. He couldn't help noticing that the red-and-black raspberry bushes were loaded with berries. The area he chose to hide in gave him a good vantage point, for he could see a good distance. As the rustling kept coming closer to him, he wondered if it might be the bear, so he took his colt out of its holster. Closer and closer the rustling came, and all he could see was a young Indian maiden, giddy and oblivious to everything around her. Apparently, she was all alone, for he could not see anyone else.

She was right in front of him and did not notice him until he sprang forward, using one hand to cover her mouth to prevent her from screaming. As she began to claw and kick him, he grabbed his big red handkerchief, stuffed it in her mouth, and wrestled her to the ground. After rolling her over and sitting on her back, he took his blue bandana, placed it over her mouth to keep the red handkerchief in, and tied it in a knot at the back of her head. He took two pieces of lashing and tied her hands behind her and also her feet. All she could do was roll around on the ground now, so Salvador left to load the last barrel of water on the mule.

The barrels all secure on the mule now, all Salvador could think of was revenge, for they had taken his Angelita from him. Now he intended to get even by taking one of theirs. He picked up the young maiden, draped her over the mule between the two sets of barrels, tied her securely, and set off back up to the arroyo and back to the camp with her kicking the mule in its side all the way.

As he arrived back at the camp, the others saw the extra cargo he had brought.

Tomas said, "This will surely bring the Comanches on us."

Andres said, "Now we will be dead by morning."

Juan said, "Salvador, you have lost your mind," and Antonio said, "My poor mule, its ribs will be sore for a month of Sundays."

While all this was going on, Salvador placed her under the seat of the covered wagon and loaded the water barrels on both sides of the wagon.

With the mule hitched to the other wagon, Salvador climbed up in the seat of the covered wagon, and they headed west. Every five minutes, Andres and Tomas were turning around in their saddles, knowing that they would be seeing the Comanches coming after them. This they continued to do until they had traveled fifteen miles. Juan and Antonio drove the other two wagons, and though they were also nervous, they were not about to admit it to anyone. The rain began to fall as a light mist at first, but now it was a steady downpour. They had continued for another ten miles in the downpour before sunset, and now they were going to camp for the night.

They built a canopy and gathered some rocks to make a bed for the fire. They got some dry wood out of the wagon Antonio had driven. With the fire started, Salvador began to make coffee and heated up the chili. In the other skillet, he browned some pieces of meat, added some potatoes, and then broke some eggs into it. As he continued to stir everything together, Tomas was the most vocal.

"What were you thinking? Or apparently, you weren't thinking. You know that they will be looking for her. All they have to do is follow our tracks, especially after this rain."

Salvador did not say a word as he started to fill the plates with the food. Once they had filled their coffee cups for the third time, the better part of valor was to put out the fire just to play it safe. They would be sleeping in the wagons tonight, and Salvador knew they would be on their way at first light.

He took a cup of water and set it along with a plate of food on the driver's seat of the covered wagon. Reaching below it, he pulled her out from under it and was surprised that she was not half as wet as they were. He lifted her up over the seat and put her in the back of the wagon. There, he sat her up, untied the blue bandana, and took out the red handkerchief. She did not scream out, to his amazement; so he reached around, took a spoonful of food out of the plate, and gave it to her. She opened her mouth, took in the food, and just as fast spit it into Salvador's face, unleashing a bloodcurdling scream. Salvador soaked the red handkerchief in the cup of water and stuffed it back in her mouth. Once again, the blue bandana was over her mouth and tied behind her head. Salvador wiped his face as he looked in her eyes and said, "Eres desgraciada." (You are ungrateful.) He then laid her on the floor of the wagon, making her as comfortable as he could, and covered her with a blanket. He changed into a dry shirt and draped a blanket around his shoulders. The rain had stopped before they ate supper; and now, as he sat in the driver's seat, he listened to her as she thrashed around in the back of the wagon until she finally fell asleep from exhaustion.

*****

Salvador awoke an hour earlier than usual and began to make a fire to cook breakfast and make coffee, with the blanket still wrapped around his shoulders, for the morning air had an extra chill to it because of the rain last night. Already he could tell that today the sun would shine brightly. Even though it was still dark, he woke the others because the coffee and breakfast were ready. While they sat there warming themselves by the fire, drinking their coffee, and eating their breakfast, Tomas started again. Antonio told him to ease off.

"Can't you see that Salvador now has a mountain lion by the tail?"

Tomas stated, "Sí [yes], but that puma [cougar] could cause us all to be scalped."

The men had finished eating and drinking their coffee when Salvador gathered the cups and dishes and said, "Let's mount up and get started. I can do the dishes when we stop again."

Chapter 6

Screech Owl

They had traveled five miles before she woke up and struggled to get into a sitting position. Salvador did not pay attention to her as he continued to drive the team. As she sat there, she was so mad at herself because no one could have captured her had she not been so giddy and oblivious yesterday. That morning, her father had told her that she had been promised to Little Pony, the youngest son of Chief Tabequeva (Sun Eagle). Even though they would have to wait until the leaves fell the next year, she was so happy, for she had been hoping for this for a year now. Her throat was becoming dry, so she began to suck on the red handkerchief to get moisture down her throat.

What was to become of her now that this man who spoke the *yuhu taibo tekwapv* (Spanish language) had captured her? She had been raised to fear the Spaniards because they would rape and dismember all female captives and feed them to their dogs, but he had not touched her yet. She knew for certain in her heart that Little Pony would be gathering warriors to come and rescue her, and she must will herself to live until she was rescued.

They stopped when the sun was center in the sky, and to their surprise, they had already covered about twenty miles. Juan made the fire while Antonio began to peel potatoes; and Andres and Tomas fed, watered, and groomed the animals. Salvador made the masa (dough) for the tortillas, and while they were cooking, he took some of the strips of buffalo meat they had cut into jerky and cut it up, adding it to the potatoes and chili that Antonio was cooking. As he continued to make tortillas, he took another strip of jerky and waited until all the potatoes had been dished up before placing it in the skillet to fry it. Once everyone had finished eating, Salvador went back to the wagon with a cup of water and the strip of jerky he had fried.

Her throat was still very dry, and when she saw Salvador coming with the cup of water, her throat seemed to become completely dry. Salvador entered the wagon and motioned to her that he would take the bandana and the red handkerchief off if she did not scream. Of course, Salvador had no way of knowing if she understood him, but he reached around her head and took off the bandana. She opened her mouth, and he reached in to take the red handkerchief out, thinking that she would bite him. To his amazement, he did not get bitten, nor did she scream. He then began to feed her the water. Half the cup was gone when he took out his knife. She tried to move away from him, thinking he was going to kill her, until she saw that he was cutting the piece of jerky into smaller pieces. He placed the first piece in her mouth, and it was still warm as she began to chew. After the second piece, he gave her the rest of the water, then went with the cup to get her more water. He returned and continued to feed her the rest of the jerky and two more cups of water.

With almuerzo (lunch) over, they broke camp, washed the utensils, and hitched the animals to the wagons. Now they needed to alter their course to a more southwesterly direction. As they traveled, the noise of the wagons approaching would at different intervals send the *codornices* (quail) in flight, making such a racket that Andres and Tomas would almost jump out of their saddles each time, for they still expected to see the Comanches coming after them.

The animals maintained a steady pace as if they knew they were on their way home. They had traveled an additional fifteen miles that afternoon before they stopped under a lone cottonwood tree to make camp as dusk was approaching. Everyone went about getting everything ready and taking care of the animals. Salvador prepared *cena* (supper), and after everyone had eaten, they sat around the campfire enjoying their coffee.

Yesterday and today, she had kept looking out the back of the covered wagon in hopes she could see signs of Little Pony coming to rescue her; however, she had not seen any, and now she began to wonder if she would ever be rescued. Hope began to dwindle as she started to shed tears.

They sat in front of the fire drinking their coffee, all relaxed, when all at once, a mournful wailing sound came, followed by two plaintive, tremulous whistles. Everyone jumped and started to look around, then Salvador said, "Look up in the tree. You can see the yellow eyes and the prominent ear tufts."

Up on a branch, a screech owl was perched.

Tomas, the self-proclaimed historian and the most superstitious of them all, said, "You all know that when you hear the call of the screech owl, someone is going to die."

The owl just kept screeching, and you could almost see the hair stand up on the back of Tomas's neck each time it screeched. They picked the order they would keep watch, and the others went to bed.

<h1 style="text-align:center">Chapter 7</h1>

<h1 style="text-align:center">Purgatoire River</h1>

Tomas was still awake and talking to Juan, who had the last watch, when Salvador awoke and began to get everything ready for breakfast. The last of the bacon was frying, the potatoes and chili were in different skillets, and the coffee was brewing while Salvador continued to make enough tortillas. The bacon finished frying, and Salvador began to fry the eggs in the bacon grease. As the eggs finished, they all dished up their plates and filled their coffee cups.

Salvador left the area by the campfire and went back to the wagon with water and a plate of eggs, potatoes, bacon, and two tortillas. Placing the plate on the floor at the back of the wagon, he climbed in and sat on her legs. He pulled out the horse shackles, which he had wrapped with cloth, from the toolbox at the end of the wagon. Then he took out his knife and cut off the lashings on her ankles, rubbed some salve on her ankles, and put the horse shackles on her feet. At least with the horse shackles wrapped, they would not injure her feet. He got off her legs, turned her around, and, cut off the lashings at her wrists with his knife. He then handed her the plate and tortillas and placed the cup of water on top of the toolbox.

Salvador went back to join the others, and they were all telling Tomas that he was too superstitious for his own good and should have gotten some sleep last night because now, if the Comanches came after them, they were going to find him asleep on his horse. They had two more cups of coffee before the pot was empty, and

once everything was put away, they started on a more westerly direction to meet the Purgatoire River, where its northern flow turned
sharply to the east for about ten miles before making another sharp
turn to continue north.

All saddled and ready to roll, they headed out. Mile after mile
they rode, Andres and Tomas on their horses and the others in the
wagons. The further the sun rose in the sky, the hotter the day
became, and the higher the dust would rise.

Salvador glanced back and noticed that she was directly behind
him. He placed his left hand on the seat, indicating that she could sit
up there with him if she wanted. She sat backward on the seat and
swung her legs around as she had the horse shackles on. They continued in silence, mile after mile.

Today they would not stop for lunch because they wanted to
cross the Purgatoire before dusk. The sun was high overhead when
she began to giggle quietly to herself. After the second time, Salvador
looked over at her with an inquisitive look. She noticed him looking
at her and pointed at Tomas, who was riding ahead and to the right
of them. She had been watching how his head kept bending forward
to his chest and then snapping back. He would shake his head and
ride almost rigid until his head began to bob again. They continued
to watch him as he fell asleep on his horse until they both broke out
in laughter when Tomas fell sound asleep and fell off his horse on
the left side, landing on the ground with an awakening jolt. He was
lucky that his horse was not spooked, and he was able to catch up
with it in a few steps and remount.

With Tomas now wide awake, they could see the narrow ribbon
of trees and bushes that grew along both sides of the Purgatoire River
off in the distance, and they would be there in a few hours.

*****

They arrived at the river and continued west until it turned
south. Now they were looking for the best location to ford the river
and get to the other side, where the Santa Fe Trail was, to make camp
for the night. A location was found; and one by one, they crossed the

river and traveled about another mile before they stopped to make camp. Salvador began to prepare the food while the others fixed a wheel on Antonio's wagon and then fed and watered the animals.

Supper was prepared, and there was enough for everyone to have a big portion. Since they did not have lunch, everyone, including the cougar (as all of them except for Salvador referred to her), had seconds. Their stomachs full, they put on another pot of coffee as they settled around the fire, drinking what they still had in their cups. The coffee finished boiling as the sun hid behind the horizon when a horde of mosquitoes descended upon them. Now that they were three days' journey away from the area they knew the Comanches were in, even Andres and Tomas felt secure enough to put dried buffalo chips on the fire to chase the mosquitoes away.

Salvador, swatting the mosquitoes constantly as they landed on him, knew that the cougar also must be getting eaten alive. As soon as the buffalo chips began to burn and chase the mosquitoes away, Salvador got up, went to the wagon, picked her up in his arms, and took her back with him to the campfire. He sat her down near him. Everyone was filling their cups with coffee again; and Salvador filled another cup, added a teaspoon of sugar to it, and handed it to her. They sat there, listening to the river as it flowed to the north. They talked, drank their coffee, and enjoyed the peace from the mosquitoes that the buffalo chips had brought them until they each, one by one, headed off to get some sleep.

Salvador had prepared buffalo steaks, eggs, chili, and tortillas for breakfast and also had a big pot of pinto beans cooking, which he planned to have for lunch. He had also made two apple pies in his *horno* (Dutch oven) from the dried apples he had and planned to have them as a surprise at supper.

He had the last watch last night, which had given him plenty of time to fix everything. He let everyone sleep late that morning and now had to wake everyone up to eat breakfast before it got cold. Everything tasted so good, and the coffee hit the spot as they took their time; now that they were on the Santa Fe Trail and with luck on their side, they would be home in four days.

The sun was up about ten degrees on the horizon when they started on their way south on the Santa Fe Trail, following the Purgatoire River. They traveled at a leisurely pace, keeping their eyes on the Sangre de Cristo (Blood of Christ) Mountains, as they planned to camp at the foothills of the mountains today. Mile after mile, they traveled until the sun was overhead. They stopped just long enough to fry potatoes, make chili, and heat up the beans. After they had eaten, they continued on their way.

Now she rode up front with Salvador as they continued toward the mountains, still following the river on their left side. After traveling for two hours, the Santa Fe Trail made a gradual turn to a southwesterly direction. As they continued through what seemed to be an endless expanse of short grass prairie, Salvador jerked and acted surprised when she expelled gas, for the beans were doing their magic. He looked at her, and she was blushing.

He said, "¿Qué pasó?" (What happened?) and began to laugh.

After another two hours on the trail, where it turned up a hill just before the Purgatoire River and headed south along Gallinas Creek, Salvador expelled gas. It took him a moment to realize that she had said, "¿Qué pasó?" and they were both still laughing when they stopped to make camp near the creek.

There were still about four hours of sunlight left as they took care of the animals and began to make the campfire. Salvador started to peel potatoes and planned to make mashed potatoes, a new batch of chili, tortillas, buffalo steaks, and, of course, the apple pies he had baked that morning.

Chapter 8

Prairie Flower

Juan then said, "There are three men on horseback with pack mules coming off the pass."

They prepared themselves just in case there might be trouble. Salvador saw them coming and continued with his cooking. As the three riders came within two hundred yards of their camp, Salvador looked out again and recognized one of the riders as Manuel Avila, a well-known hunter and trapper who knew at least seven different Indian languages. He had met Manuel at Bent's Fort three years before. When they arrived, Salvador greeted them and told them they were just in time for supper and invited them to spend the night.

Once everything was done, Salvador fixed a plate of steak and mashed potatoes with the first piece of pie. He did not tell the others about the pie. Once he had taken it to her in the wagon, he went back and began to serve everyone their steaks as they helped themselves to the mashed potatoes and chili. As soon as everyone had finished their steak and potatoes, Salvador put on a second pot of coffee. After a few minutes, as the men were talking about Salvador's cougar, the coffee began to boil over into the fire. Salvador removed the coffee pot and began to fill all their coffee cups. Then he asked, "Who wants a piece of apple pie?" They all grabbed their plates and got in line as Salvador gave each a slice. After everyone had gotten a slice, he then let them know that there was enough for seconds.

Salvador and Manuel had finished their apple pie and were enjoying their coffee when Salvador asked Manuel to teach him some Comanche words. Manuel told Salvador that he would, but first, he wanted to go see his cougar. They walked over together, and as they arrived, Manuel, speaking in Comanche, introduced himself and said, "Nv nahnia tsa Manuel Avila. Vnha hakai nahniaka?" (My name is Manuel Avila. What is your name?)

"Nv nahnia tsa Totsiyaa" (My name is Totsiyaa), she responded and continued to tell him how she acquired her name. She told Manuel that when she was born, her mother said that she was as beautiful as the wildflowers that bloom in the spring, and that is why she was named Totsiyaa, or Prairie Flower.

Manuel then asked, "Vnha hvv tomopv?" (How old are you?)

To this, Prairie Flower responded, "To-ach'chv-wit[e]-ma-toi-kut" (Seventeen).

Manuel continued to talk with her for about thirty minutes. When he finished his cup of coffee, he stated to her, "Salvador tis'che-woon'ie" (Salvador looks ugly), to which she replied, "Ka cha-na'woonit" (No, good looking).

Manuel laughed and told Salvador, "Let's go get another cup of coffee and some pie."

They refilled their cups with coffee and sat down by the fire to eat their pie. Manuel began to tell everyone that the puma's name was Prairie Flower and that she had been betrothed to the youngest son of Chief Tabequeva. A puzzled look came over his face as he told them how lucky they were because Chief Tabequeva would have sent out a war party immediately unless he thought that she might have been eaten by a grizzly.

Salvador asked Manuel what was said when his name was used in the conversation with Prairie Flower.

Manuel explained that he had called him ugly, and she said that he was good-looking.

They finished eating their pie, and true to his word, Manuel began to have Salvador repeat after him, "Hakai_nvvmv nahniakai?" (What's the Comanche word for _____?). Then Manuel had Salvador repeat the phrase each time he wanted to learn a word.

Salvador got the phrase correct, and the first words he wanted to learn were *please (haamee)*, *thank you (vra)*, *yes (haa)*, *no (kee)*, *hello (marvawe)*. He also wanted to know how to say "How are you?" (Vnha hakai nvvsvka?) and "Fine, and you?" (Tsaatv, vntse?).

Manuel said, "Hold on, my friend. Learn what you know right now because if you have too much, you will forget everything."

They sat there by the fire enjoying a third cup of coffee and talking of bygone days.

Salvador got up, did the dishes, put them away, then joined Manuel again and said, "Let's see if I remember what the teacher taught me," and began to go over the phrases and words he had learned.

"Very good, my friend," Manuel said as they both said good night and went to their bed rolls and went to bed.

Salvador lay on top of his bedroll and began to repeat all the phrases and words over and over until he fell asleep. He awoke at his normal time but woke up tired this morning. Nevertheless, he began to prepare breakfast of potatoes, chili, buffalo strips, and eggs. The coffee began to boil, and Salvador moved it to the side as he continued cooking.

Antonio and Andres had gotten up, and when Andres told Antonio, "Buenos días. Que Dios le dé un buen día. ¿Cómo amaneció?" (Good morning, May God give you a good day. How did you wake up?), Antonio said, "Acostado" (Lying down). They both laughed, which awoke the others.

Everyone ate breakfast and finished off the coffee. As dawn broke and now with daylight, Manuel and his companions said their thanks and best wishes before departing on their way north.

Chapter 9

The Pass

Salvador finished washing the plates, cups, and skillets, then went and hitched the team to the wagon. After making sure everything was put away and secure, he entered the wagon through the back and took the horse shackles off Prairie Flower. He went back out and made sure everyone was ready to move out.

Today was going to be the hardest part of the journey because the Mountain Branch of the Santa Fe Trail followed along Gallinas Creek as it started its way up the pass. They lined up the wagons in single file: Andres went ahead of the first wagon with Juan at the reins, then Antonio behind him, with Salvador next and Tomas bringing up the rear.

The first two wagons, with almost six thousand pounds in each of them and about four thousand pounds in Salvador's wagon, now began the steady climb through the narrow defile filled with boulders and sudden turns that gave glimpses of the green valley below. There was constant communication from front to back as every sixty yards, there were large boulders or steep little hillocks that had to be traversed.

Hours passed as they went higher and higher, driving their teams and making their wagons crawl along the edge of steep drop-offs to pass overhanging rocks. Four hours later, Juan finally reached the summit of the pass. As previously planned, Andres tethered his horse behind Juan's wagon and climbed aboard just in case additional help was needed with the brakes on the wagon during the descent.

Tomas rode cautiously past Salvador on the left side along the edge of a steep drop-off. Reaching Antonio's wagon, he climbed on and tethered his horse in the back as the wagon made the summit and began its way down the pass.

Reaching the summit, Salvador made the sign of the cross and said a short prayer of thanksgiving for having had a safe journey so far. Everyone was still communicating to the back as they came upon hazards on the trail during the descent. Now at least it was easier on the animals, and the hardest part in some areas was to use the brakes to keep the wagons behind the animals.

It took four hours to reach the summit; and now, almost two hours on the descent, they could see Willow Springs. They arrived at Willow Springs, which was nothing more than a spring that fed a few ponds and was an area used often by all those who traveled the Santa Fe Trail to replenish their water supply and water their stock. They decided to camp for the night to allow the animals to rest after such a hard trip over the pass.

They took care of the animals, groomed them, and then fed and watered them. They also made sure that all their legs were okay. Now they had the rest of the afternoon to just relax, having had a light lunch. The day was hot, and after an hour, Tomas said he was going to one of the ponds that were fed by the spring and go swimming to cool off. The others thought it was a great idea and went to the pond with Tomas; they all stripped down to their underwear and jumped in.

Prairie Flower could not see them but could hear them laughing and splashing around as she looked in the direction they were. Salvador noticed the expression on her face and motioned for her to come and follow him. They arrived at another pond about a hundred yards from them, and he motioned to her that she could go swimming in that pond. She was hesitant because she thought Salvador would also be going in, but he motioned for her to go ahead and turned his back to the pond. She felt comfortable now, for she knew that he would keep watch. She made it down to the edge of the pond, went behind one of the bushes that encircled the pond, took off her buckskin dress, and dove naked into the pond. She enjoyed the swim so much that an hour went by before she got out and put on her buckskin dress again.

She walked up behind Salvador, poked him in the back, and motioned for him to go ahead and swim.

Salvador took her advice and went for a swim. After about thirty minutes, he walked up to her as she had finished putting her hair in two braids. Salvador then said in Comanche, "Hakai_____nvmv nahniaka?" as he touched her braids.

She said, "Wvhtamv."

Salvador repeated the word a couple of times to help himself remember it. She then got his attention and, holding one of her braids in one hand, pointed to his mouth.

He realized that she wanted to know the Spanish word for braids. Salvador told her it was *trenzas*, and she repeated it back to him to make sure she was saying it correctly.

They walked back to the wagon as they each began to realize that they were starting to communicate with each other. On the way back, she realized that he knew how to ask for the Comanche word for something, and she wanted to know how to ask for the Spanish word. She asked him in Comanche and pointed to his mouth again, and he asked her, "¿Qué es la palabra en español?" She repeated the phrase all the way back to the wagon; and when they each got a cup of water, she stuck her finger in the cup, swirled the water, pointed to it and said, "Pah," then asked him in Spanish for the word, to which he replied, "Agua." She was happy with herself, for now she would make the best out of a bad situation and planned on learning his language.

After a few hours, Salvador began to make supper while the others took buckets and went to where the artesian spring came out of the ground. They filled their buckets and poured them into the barrels that were empty. They finished filling the barrels just as supper was ready to be dished up. They got their plates and began to fill them out of the big pot, for Salvador had made a stew. Salvador handed Prairie Flower a plate and got one for himself; he had her fill her plate first and then he served himself. They sat around the fire, with Prairie Flower seated next to Salvador as they ate their meal. The men talked, reliving their trip up the pass and joking with each other.

Prairie Flower finished eating the food on her plate, left it on the stone she had been sitting on, and went back to the covered wagon. She prepared her area to lie down, began to unbraid her hair, yawned, and lay down. She felt so good, having had a chance to bathe herself, being able now to communicate, and having a full stomach, and now she felt more comfortable around Salvador and was not afraid of him anymore. She settled in, covered herself, and drifted off to sleep.

Salvador began to do the dishes, and Antonio was drying them as fast as he handed them to him while they continued to talk about the next day's trip. They planned to head out early and would decide whether or not to leave the Santa Fe Trail when they arrived at that point on the trail where it made its way to Cimarron. With everything put away, they decided to turn in early and get some well-deserved rest.

Chapter 10

Mouth on Fire

Salvador had the last watch and started, as usual, to get everything ready for breakfast. Then he began to make tortillas while he fried a double batch of potatoes and jerky meat. Dawn was just beginning to break when he began to make burritos. He took a tortilla and laid it on the table, and then with a big spoon of chili, he began to spread it over the entire tortilla. He placed four strips of fried buffalo jerky in the center, side by side, then a spoon of potatoes on top of the jerky. Taking the bottom of the tortilla, he folded about a quarter of it up over the potatoes and jerky, then took the left side of the tortilla and brought it up over the ingredients. Holding everything together, he continued to roll the tortilla with the ingredients until all the tortilla was wrapped, making a tube or pocket filled with the jerky and potatoes. After making four, he took a towel, laid it on the table, and placed the burritos in the center, stacking them one on top of the other. He then wrapped the towel around them securely and tied the towel with twine as if it were a present.

He continued to make enough burritos until he had five bundles. He would give each person a bundle, and as they went on their journey today, they would not have to stop for lunch. The others had already fed and watered the animals and had taken buckets to the artesian spring that created Willow Springs. They had made four trips, and now the two empty water barrels were full. As daybreak arrived, Salvador began to fry eggs; and as soon as they were done, everyone began to fill their plates.

Once everyone had finished eating, they began to harness, saddle, and hitch the animals to the wagons as Salvador cleaned and dried all the plates, cups, and skillets and the coffeepot. He then took the dishwater, put out the campfire, and climbed up into the driver's seat of the covered wagon; and they headed south on the Santa Fe Trail, leaving Willow Springs behind them.

They had traveled about five miles when Prairie Flower climbed over the seat and joined Salvador up front. They continued to travel south for about ten more miles, and then they decided to leave the Santa Fe Trail and continue traveling south. At that point, the Santa Fe Trail went southwest towards the mountains, but they knew that it made almost an elongated half-circle and turned south again. They planned to cut a day off the journey by going straight and would join back up with the Santa Fe Trail again when the mountain and the prairie trails joined together, for both trails were the Santa Fe Trail.

Prairie Flower had been very quiet for the last two hours when she tapped Salvador on the left shoulder to get his attention. Holding her head with both hands, one on either side, she said, "Paapi" (Comanche), then told Salvador "¿Qué es?" to which he replied "Cabeza." They both repeated the respective words a few times, then she continued by pointing or gesturing, starting with *eye (puil ojo)*, *ear (nakil oído)*, *nose (muubil nariz)*, mouth *(tvvpil boca)*, arm *(aamal brazo)*, *chest (nvnapvl pecho)*, *heart (pihil corazón)*, *stomach (sapvl estómago)*, *hand (mo?ol mano)*, *knee (tanapvl rodilla)*, *foot (naapel pie)*, and *ankle bone (kotsuok?otsune hueso del tobillo)*. Having repeated each word two or three times, they now paused as if to memorize each one.

Time and distance had passed so quickly as they taught each other, for now the sun was overhead. Salvador pointed to the bundle on the floor and motioned for her to pick it up and place it between them on the seat. While she was picking up the bundle, he hooked the reins on the brake handle and began to unwrap the bundle. He then handed her a burrito and took one for himself. She watched as he took the open end of the burrito, stuck it in his mouth, took a big bite, and began to chew. She did the same, and after chewing it, she swallowed fast and said, "*Oooh*, Salvador, kotopv," while pointing at the ingredients of the burrito, because her mouth was on fire now. She grabbed the canteen and took a big swallow of water before continuing to eat the burrito, only now she took smaller bites.

Salvador was so surprised that she had said his name but kept wondering as he took another bite of his burrito what she had tried to tell him because he had never heard *kotopv* before. They finished eating the burritos and had traveled about five miles when Tomas and Andres halted their horses and waited for Salvador to drive up between them.

Tomas told Salvador that they were going to ride ahead and find a place to ford the Canadian River. With that said, Tomas let out a yell, spurred his horse, and took off at full speed, and Andres did the same. Now, as if on a racecourse, Tomas in the lead and Andres trying to catch him, they continued until all that could be seen was the dust they left behind.

Silently they continued their way south, except that Prairie Flower kept touching different parts of her body. Without realizing it, as she touched a part, Salvador was repeating the Comanche word for it in his mind. This continued for a long while as he realized that she had been doing the same thing, only in Spanish.

All at once, Prairie Flower began to bark like a dog, then said the Comanche word *sarii*, and Salvador responded, "Perro." She then howled like a coyote and said, "Kvtseena," and he replied, "Coyote." As she pointed to the sun and made a circle with her hands, she said, "Taabe," and he said "Sol." She was very explicit with gestures and continued with *man (tenahpv/hombre)*, *woman (wa'ipv/mujer)*, *moon (mva/luna)*, cat *(wa?oo/gato)*, *bird (huutsuu/pájaro)*, and then *good (tsaatv/bueno)*. Then Prairie Flower said *pe'a-hock-soiv'woon-it* as she pointed up into the sky, for there was a big bald eagle soaring aloft. They stopped repeating words when they could see Tomas and Andres riding back toward them.

"Estamos con suerte" (We are in luck), Tomas said. "The river is very low, and I would guess it has not rained in two months."

Tomas and Andres turned their horses around and led the way to where they would cross the river.

Once they crossed the river, they continued for two more hours. In the distance, Salvador could see a mountain to the southeast that resembled a wagon being pulled by oxen. They stopped to make camp for the night.

The sun was hidden behind a cloud, making a brilliant-red sunset. Andres made the fire while the others took care of the animals and packed grease in the rear wheels of Juan's wagon.

Prairie Flower was beside Salvador as he began to make supper. Still thinking of the word *kotopv* that she had used that afternoon, he repeated the word to her, and she pointed to the fire that Andres had made. He smiled to himself, for now he understood what she had meant. With some of the food already cooking, Salvador began to make chili when Prairie Flower pointed at the chili and said, "Kotopv. Kee." (Spicy. No.)

He responded in Comanche and said, "Chile," the Spanish word for chili.

As he got the plates, he began to give her the Spanish word for each item: *plate, plato*; *knife, cuchillo*; *fork, tenedor*; *spoon, cuchara*; *skillet, sartén*; and *towel, toalla.*" Then, when he picked up his cup to drink some coffee, she said, "Aawo" as she touched the cup, and he told her it was a *taza.*

*****

It was dusk now, and everyone had eaten their fill when Salvador got up to do the dishes and Prairie Flower followed him. As he stacked the dishes, he began to tell them how he had forgotten not to put chili in Prairie Flower's burritos; and when they ate them, she wanted to know how he had put fire in them. They all began to laugh as he washed the first plate and Prairie Flower took the *plato* and began to dry it.

"Teach her right, cuñado [brother-in-law]," Juan said as they watched her dry the plates.

"Did you see that?" Andres asked when Prairie Flower handed back a plate that still had some chili on it.

"It looks to me like she is going to teach him how to do them right," said Antonio, and again they all laughed.

After the dishes were all done and put away, they sat back down, and the men continued to talk while drinking their coffee. Prairie Flower enjoyed her coffee with sugar.

While she was drinking her coffee, she kept going over the phrase "buenas noches," which they always said to one another before they went to bed, and felt certain she would say it correctly, for she had heard it each night.

When she had finished her cup of coffee, she got up, stood in front of Antonio, and said, "Buenas noches, Antonio," and continued around the fire, telling each of them by name. Once she finished telling Salvador, she began to walk to the covered wagon.

They responded, "Buenas noches" together because they had been awestruck and amazed.

Prairie Flower reached the covered wagon with a smile on her face and went to bed.

The men, still in shock, looked at one another as Tomas said, "What all have you been teaching her, Salvador?"

"Teaching her! I think it is more like she is teaching me," said Salvador.

They all laughed and began to get ready for bed.

Chapter 11

Hermit Monk

They broke camp early that morning and had been heading south for over two hours now. The mountain that resembled a wagon being pulled by oxen was now to the northeast of them as they watched a herd of short-prong antelope grazing to their left, undaunted by their approach.

In another hour, they would connect with the eastern branch of the Santa Fe Trail; and shortly after, the eastern branch would join with the Cimarron branch of the Santa Fe Trail. Then the trail would become one as it continued south.

The fork of the trail where the two became one was now behind them as they continued south. There would be no lunch today because they would arrive at Nuestra Señora de los Dolores de Las Vegas (Our Lady of Sorrows of the Meadows) while the sun was still high in the sky. Las Vegas was the last Spanish colony established, consisting of thirty families in a fortified enclosure with a large plaza in the center.

Making camp in the plaza among the others who were heading either north or south, Salvador stayed with the wagons as the others went about town to see what was new and get a beer.

Tomas came back early, and he had with him an old copy of the *American Beacon* newspaper. He found a nice shady spot under a tall tree, sat down, and began to read it.

When the others returned, they handed Salvador the bag of candy he had asked them to pick up for Marcelino. They also had a box full of empty bottles they had purchased and shared them with everyone.

The box contained bottles of different sizes, in different colors, and even some empty whiskey bottles. It was well known that the traders would drink the whiskey on the trail and still make a profit selling the empty whiskey bottles because the bottles could be used for many different things. Once everyone had the bottles they wanted, Antonio walked over to Prairie Flower, reached in his pocket, pulled out a four-inch bottle that shimmered in many different colors, and gave it to her.

She said, "Vva" (Thank you).

While they sat and ate that night, Tomas began to tell them that two men named Andrew Jackson and Martin Van Buren were running against each other to become president of the United States and that a lady named Victoria in London, England, in Europe, had become queen last month. He then told them that there were some men from Tejas (Texas) wanting the president of the United States to recognize Tejas as a republic.

"What difference does it make to us?" asked Andres. "We are still under the rule of Anastasio Bustamante."

"It is important," Tomas said, "because things as we know them are going to change so rapidly in the next few years."

There in the shade of the tree, they continued to discuss the news and politics of the day for over an hour when Salvador told them that he and Prairie Flower were going to pay his respects to Don Miguel Romero. Don Miguel Romero was already becoming a prominent merchant in Las Vegas and was a very good friend of Salvador's family, especially his uncle Santiago. Though Don Romero was no relation, Salvador had always called him *tío* (uncle).

About the same time the year before, a band of Navajos had kidnapped Luis and Manuel Montoya, who were nephews of his uncle. Upon hearing the news, Don Miguel Romero immediately volunteered to go on an expedition to rescue them. His uncle had told him how they had tracked the Navajos for many days, crisscrossing the Santa Fe Trail and finally rescuing the boys somewhere in Kansas.

Upon their return, and before leaving Kansas, they had met a religious mystic, a monk that everyone had heard of because it was said that he had the gift of healing people and was a hermit. They had been invited to his cave and had a meal of coarse cornmeal, milk, and water, for that was all the monk lived on. His cave was not much bigger than four feet by four feet. In talking to the monk, they found out that he was a son of a prosperous Italian family and, since he became a monk, devoted all his time to prayer and religious duties. It was hard for them to envision how a person could live on coarse cornmeal and in such a small cave, but when they found out that before coming to Kansas, the monk had lived in a hollow tree somewhere in Missouri. Upon their departure, he had given them his blessing for a safe journey back home.

Arriving at Don Miguel Romero's home, they were greeted and immediately asked to stay for supper. Salvador introduced Prairie Flower and greeted his *tío* and *tía*, conveying the best wishes of his uncle and the others. Their house had twenty-three rooms that formed a courtyard (*placita*) and had a complete portal decorated with painted flowers and grapes. Their house was in the northern part of the enclosure, which was Las Vegas. In talking with his *tío*, Salvador found out that this was going to be the last year that the Romero family would spend the winter in Santa Fe; the business was picking up, and the town had over a thousand residents. They had supper and continued talking, exchanging all the news of the families since they had last seen each other.

Salvador gave his thanks for supper and the conversation and excused himself because he wanted to join the others and get an early start the next morning. Arriving back at the plaza, they joined up with the others and sat around the campfire for almost two hours before everyone went to bed, to get an early start. The next day, they would be home before suppertime.

Chapter 12

Chonita

They were all up just before sunrise, had a quick breakfast, broke camp, and headed toward the south gate of the Las Vegas plaza. Passing the merchants on both sides of the street that purchased the wool (*lana*) and hides (*cueros*) during shearing time, they continued down the street. They passed houses built in the Spanish style of architecture in L, U, or complete square shapes, forming *placitas* in the rear of their homes, while the front of each house only had a small portal or just a simple doorway. Out the south gate, they proceeded and headed toward Romeoville and, from there, onward to their community.

Once they arrived at their community, they stopped at each casa or rancho, sharing the meat in the wagons, making sure the widows in the area had plenty. As they progressed from place to place, they used the meat out of Antonio's wagon because he and Andres would be the first to arrive home in Chappell.

The three continued on until Tomas left them in Serafina. Then Juan got home about ten miles southeast of Serafina, in El Ojito, where they loaded additional meat into Salvador's wagon for all the stops he would make on the way to his home in La Lagunita.

Salvador, now at the last stop, climbed off the wagon and greeted his brother Gregorio as Marcelino came running and jumped into his arms. Once they finished unloading Gregorio's share of meat for his family, Gregorio asked Salvador about the Indian. Salvador reminded him of how he felt before the trip and the reasons for the capture of the Indian.

"But did you do the right and honorable thing?" Gregorio asked before Salvador headed home.

With Marcelino seated between them, Salvador said, "Dar le la mano" (implying to shake hands with her). He pointed to her and said, "Totsiyaa," then pointed to and said, "Marcelino," as he looked at her. They both had trouble saying each other's names, so Prairie Flower began to say her name slowly until Marcelino said it correctly, then Marcelino did the same.

When the wagon stopped at the back of the house, Marcelino crawled over Prairie Flower and climbed down, raising his hand to her as he motioned for her to get down. Once she did, he took her by the hand and almost pulled her into the house. Salvador unloaded and put away the meat, then went back out to put away the wagon and take care of the animals. Marcelino showed Prairie Flower every room in the house, then took her outside, still pulling her as he showed her all around the ranch. Salvador, having tended to all the animals, picked some ears of sweet corn, zucchini, and bell peppers, then returned to the house to make supper. He chopped the bell peppers into small pieces, cut the corn off the cob, diced the zucchini, and fried all the ingredients together.

Once everything was done, he looked out the door and hollered for Marcelino and Prairie Flower to come and eat. While they ate, he smiled to himself as he watched Marcelino trying to teach Prairie Flower how to make a scoop with the tortilla and fill it with another piece of tortilla. He told Marcelino that Prairie Flower would be sleeping in his room and that Marcelino would sleep with him. Once they had finished eating and the dishes were put away, he handed Marcelino the bag of candy. Marcelino reached in, pulled out two pieces, handed one to Prairie Flower, and then put the rest of the bag away in the drawer of the china cabinet.

*****

Each day passed with Prairie Flower helping Marcelino with his chores and taking time to play with him.

Sunday came, and Salvador did not go to church but was busy cooking in the kitchen when the others got up. He was preparing enough food for thirty people because he knew the news of his cougar had spread throughout the community.

He had just finished setting up a long table in the shade of the cottonwood tree when people started arriving. The first arrivals were Juan, Andres, Tomas, Jose, and the entire community, including all their family members and children. Antonio and his wife, Maria Concepcion (whom everyone in the community called Chonita), arrived last. As Chonita got out of the surrey, she scolded Salvador for not going to church.

"But I was busy preparing for you," he said.

"That is no excuse," she replied, grabbing her bundles of clothes, cake, and casserole, and went into the house.

The men stayed outside talking while the women took over the house, all wanting to meet Prairie Flower. The women set the table and fed the children first, then told the men to come and eat.

One by one, the families began to leave, with all the women saying *adios* (goodbye) to Prairie Flower as she stood next to Chonita, where she had been most of the day. Antonio and his family prepared to leave as Chonita told Salvador she would be back in the morning.

Chonita had been arriving each day about three hours after sunrise for the last two days. Upon her departure today, she informed Salvador that she had set aside the clothes that Prairie Flower would wear tomorrow. "I will see you in church, for you have no excuse. And after Mass, come and have lunch with us."

Sunday morning, at first light, Salvador was outside, feeding and watering the animals. Once he finished, he backed the white Arabian mare, spotted on its rear quarters, into the surrey; hitched it up; and brought it to the back of the house.

He went inside, cleaned up, got dressed, and set out the clothes for Marcelino before waking him. Marcelino and Prairie Flower were now dressed, and as they entered the kitchen, Salvador had just finished making breakfast. They ate breakfast, did the dishes, and put them away, then boarded the surrey and headed off to church.

Mass was over, and everyone made it a point to greet them and ask them over for lunch. They apologized, explaining that Chonita had already invited them the day before, but accepted each invitation, setting a date and time.

Antonio and Chonita led the way from church. With them were Antonio's father, Andres, his mother, Fransisca, and his grandfather, Don Jose Antonio, who had been a member of the Royal Spanish Calvary when stationed at the presidio in Santa Fe at Antonio's age. Salvador thought how fortunate Antonio was to still have his mother, father, and grandfather with him. He remembered that Don Jose Antonio's wife, Maria Rosa, and his parents, Jose Miguel and Catarina, all died on the same day five years ago during the cholera epidemic. Following behind Salvador were Jose, Andres, and their families, as they would all be having lunch at Antonio's.

They arrived at Antonio's, and the men took care of the animals first before coming back to sit in the shade of the porch. Antonio went inside and came out with a glass of grape wine for each of them.

When they were called in to eat, the men and women gathered around the table, and Antonio said the blessing. Before them, the table was laden with a large bowl of tossed salad with apple cider vinegar dressing, corn on the cob, mashed potatoes, white gravy, red chili, green chili peppers, fried eggplant, a pile of fried chicken, a large beef roast, and a large platter of goat meat. On the table next to the window, in the center, was a large bowl of apples and grapes, surrounded by four apple pies, four cherry pies, three pans of peach cobbler, and at least ten dozen sugar cookies.

What a feast! Everyone ate until they could eat no more, and still, Chonita was asking everyone if they wanted more. The women continued to sit at the table and talk as the men went back outside to the porch. It seemed as if, after that feast, no one could move for three hours.

<h1 style="text-align:center">Chapter 13</h1>

<h1 style="text-align:center">Thunder</h1>

Prairie Flower helped the women clean all the dishes, pots, and pans before they boarded the surrey for the ride back home after she, Salvador, and Marcelino had given their thanks for such a wonderful feast.

The rest of that month and most of the next, they met their commitment to have dinner with all the other families, either on weekdays or after church on Sunday, as previously planned. It almost seemed that each feast became larger than the one before.

Each morning, except for Sunday, Chonita would come and teach Prairie Flower all the womanly duties and Spanish, and she'd try to explain the message from the Gospel that the padre had given on Sunday. Prairie Flower learned everything so quickly that within a month, she had completely taken control of the house and now only allowed Salvador to cook occasionally.

A month and a half had passed when Salvador departed for a day to buy some horses, hoping he might be able to buy himself another palomino. At the sale, he bought six horses and had just enough for a beautiful palomino when, out of the corner of his eye, he saw a war-bonnet horse, which was a white pinto with reddish-brown markings on both sides. The markings began with an oblong circle at its rear hind quarters, then on its back behind the shoulder in the shape of a saddle and on its chest. What made it a war bonnet was the markings, which was on top of its head, down, and around the face and cheek without a break and the ears. The Indians considered this type of horse a powerful medicine horse in fighting and raids, protecting its rider from wounds.

When he arrived home the next morning, he corralled the horses except for the war bonnet, which he handed to Prairie Flower.

"Vra vra" (Thank you, thank you), she said as she mounted bareback and took off like the wind. When she returned, she thanked Salvador again and again.

Sunday arrived, and they went to church. Mass was over as the padre said, "Go with God."

Salvador thought, *Finally, a day without a commitment to someone else.* He could go home now and catch up on repairs and chores that had been neglected in the last two months.

When they arrived home, Salvador unhitched the Arabian and put away the surrey. He thought that all his life that Sundays were for rest and that one only did what had to be done, for there would be time this week to catch up on everything.

The sun was hot that afternoon as Marcelino said, "Let's go swimming," and with that suggestion, they all went inside and changed clothes. They came back out and were at the edge of the pond when Salvador picked up Marcelino and threw him in the pond, then dove in himself as Prairie Flower followed. They began to play tag; and each time she tagged Salvador, she also dunked him. After being dunked each time, Salvador would try to catch Prairie Flower to dunk her, but he would miss because she was as agile as a beaver. Only Marcelino was fast enough to tag her. Finally, after having been dunked six times, Salvador got to dunk her.

Marcelino got out of the pond. Up next to the hill was a cottonwood tree with a branch that extended over the pond. Tied to the center of the branch was a rope. The other end was tied to the base of the tree. Marcelino untied the rope from the base of the tree, climbed up a little, and swung on the rope, letting go in time to land in the water between them like a cannonball, sending water up into their faces. Prairie Flower got out of the pond and was at the tree, ready to swing in as Marcelino got out of the way. Reaching as far up on the rope as she could, she pulled back on the rope and took off over the pond. When she let go of the rope, she landed flat on her back as she hit the water and went under. Up she came, sputtering, for the landing had knocked the wind out of her. Salvador was still laughing as she splashed him on her way out to try again.

Marcelino was now coming, and he said, "Watch me. I will show you how," and into the pond he went.

The whole afternoon was spent there at the pond, just enjoying themselves.

Monday came, and with it came Chonita. He was glad she came over each day to spend time with Prairie Flower, as they kept Marcelino occupied, which allowed him the time needed to make all the necessary repairs and take care of all the animals and the garden.

A few weeks passed, and after arriving home that Sunday, Salvador unhooked the Arabian and put Marcelino's saddle on it. Then he saddled the war-bonnet and a horse for himself.

In the house, they went long enough to change clothes, and back out they came and saddled up. They headed east from the house through the apple orchard and rode for about an hour until they came to the edge of the gorge. There, they began to follow the gorge as it meandered its way southwesterly. They rode side by side along the gorge, with Salvador near the edge, Prairie Flower next to him, and Marcelino next to her. As they continued riding for about seven miles, Salvador noticed how dry the gorge was and had not seen even one pool of water in it.

They came to the area where the ridge they were on tapered downward toward a small creek, which was fed by a stream that came out about three feet below the top of the ridge. From where the stream splashed into the creek, it flowed about twenty feet before it entered the gorge. At that point, the gorge made a sharp turn and headed south. Though the stream was feeding the gorge, Salvador could see where the water ceased to flow about two hundred yards down, for the gorge was so dry.

To the right of where the gorge took an abrupt turn and headed south, Juan and his wife, Maria, were out in their garden. When Juan noticed Salvador up on the ridge, he whistled to get his attention and motioned for them to come over. Maria took off and went into the house to make coffee and something to eat, for it was a custom that whenever someone came to visit, no matter the time of day or night, you were expected to eat and have something to drink. Everyone in the community adhered to it. Prairie Flower had become used to the custom but at first thought that a person could burst if they visited too many people in one day.

As they sat around the table conversing while they ate, Sesadia, Maria's mother, said, "My knee tells me that rain is coming."

Juan and Salvador both told her they hoped she was right because it had been so dry. After a couple of hours enjoying themselves, the women cleaned and put everything away before Salvador expressed his thanks for the meal as they departed by way of the trail that led to their home.

Prairie Flower was awoken early the following morning, about three hours before sunrise, as lightning lit up the sky. She could hear the thunder in the distance and began to become fearful, for thunder was the thing she feared most. She would not be able to sleep now, so she got out of bed, wrapped a blanket around her shoulders, went into the kitchen, put some wood on the hot coals in the stove, and made a pot of coffee. Then she went into the living room and sat in front of the fireplace, watching the flames.

The lightning became brighter as the thunder grew closer and louder. With each clap of thunder, she would shudder as she sat there. She sprang to her feet and ran to Salvador's bedroom when lightning struck a tree near the house, followed by the loudest thunder she had ever heard. She lifted the covers and got into the bed next to Salvador. Almost immediately, Salvador, using his right foot and a short jab with his right fist to her upper left arm, knocked her out of the bed, and she landed on the floor beside the bed with a thud. She got up, went back into the living room, wrapped her blanket around her shoulders, and sat before the fireplace again.

The movement of the bed and the rustling of the covers when he pushed her out of the bed awoke Salvador. Now fully dressed, he walked into the living room and saw her in front of the fireplace as he went into the kitchen.

The coffee was ready, and as he poured two cups, the lightning lit everything up outside. The thunder was so loud it seemed to shake the house. Two cups in hand, he entered the living room as another thunderclap happened, and he saw Prairie Flower shudder.

He handed her a cup of coffee and sat down beside her. He took his right arm, placed it around her shoulders, and drew her next to him. They sat there in front of the fireplace until daylight, even though the thunder and lightning had ceased about an hour before.

Now it was just a light, steady rain. Prairie Flower got up and went to her room to get dressed. Salvador put on his slicker and went outside in the rain, making sure the animals were okay. Prairie Flower, now dressed, was in the kitchen making breakfast. Salvador came in, took off his slicker, and walked over to the kitchen window. He had Prairie Flower look out and see that the lightning had hit the branch of the cottonwood tree that had the rope on it, and now it was in the pond.

Chonita arrived in a light mist as Salvador was out at the pond, trying to pull the branch out. She said, "Good morning," to Salvador as she went into the house. Not ten minutes had passed as Salvador struggled with the branch when he turned around and was startled to see Chonita standing there with her arms crossed, demanding an explanation as to why Prairie Flower had a bruise on her upper left arm.

Salvador began to give her a detailed explanation, for he knew she would not accept anything less. Once Salvador finished, she turned and walked back to the house with a smile on her face as she pictured it in her mind.

The next Sunday, they spent at home doing nothing and just enjoyed each other's company.

The sun came over the horizon that Sunday morning, and Salvador already had a giant kettle suspended over the fire he had built outside, with water boiling in it. He then went into the chicken coop, caught a chicken, and held it by its feet as it cackled and fluttered its wings on its way to the chopping block by the woodpile. He placed the head of the chicken on the block, and with one swift chop of the axe, the chicken lost its head. He let the chicken go, and as it ran fluttering its wings, blood from its neck splattered everywhere. Once the chicken stopped, he picked it up, gutted it, and then put it in the kettle of boiling water.

Now began the chore he disliked the most: pulling out the chicken, then plucking off all the feathers, dunking the chicken, and plucking more feathers. He also disliked having to smell that awful odor. Once finished, he took it inside and began to cut it up into pieces, then washed each piece again before battering it and placing it in the skillet. As the chicken fried, he made breakfast while Prairie Flower set the table.

They had finished breakfast and put everything away before Salvador let them know they were going on a hike today. He took a towel, placed the fried chicken on it, and tied the opposite side corners together, leaving enough of the towel to make a handle. They climbed the hill behind the ponds and walked toward the west as Marcelino walked beside Prairie Flower, holding her hand. After they had walked for about an hour, Salvador did not pull away when Prairie Flower took his hand in hers, and they continued to walk hand in hand. After walking for three more hours, they reached a large rock outcropping on the mesa they were on. They climbed the large rock and sat to eat the chicken. Looking out to the southwest, they could see Starvation Peak, where, over a hundred years before, Indians had chased a group of early settlers to the top and starved them and all the vistas surrounding them to death. They sat there for a while after eating the chicken before climbing down off the rock outcropping. Once down, Salvador reached for Prairie Flower's hand, and she for Marcelino's, as they began their walk back home.

<h1 style="text-align:center">Chapter 14</h1>

<h1 style="text-align:center">Prized Memento</h1>

Four months had passed, and like clockwork, Chonita still arrived each day about three hours after sunrise, spending time with Prairie Flower. They had become the best of friends. Chonita would keep her informed of all the local news and teach her about God; and today she told her that Maria, Juan's wife, and Dolores, Andres's wife, were with child. Prairie Flower was so happy for them and expressed her delight, for now, they were able to speak with each other using both Spanish and Comanche.

The cottonwood trees were bare of leaves now, and the snow clouds were on the horizon. All the men—Tomas, Andres, Antonio, Juan, Salvador, and Jose—got together after Mass and planned to go on the hunt for buffalo after the gardens were planted in May.

A light, fluffy snow had fallen all day as they sat in front of the *chimenea* (fireplace) in the living room that Christmas Eve. Marcelino had become so fluent in Comanche that he used very little Spanish as he was telling Prairie Flower what to expect the next day. He explained to her that this year, they would be the last family to be serenaded by all the neighbors. They all arrived together with guitars and sang a song of celebration, "Las Mañanitas." One family would start by serenading another family, then receiving a treat and a holiday drink, and then both families would go and serenade the next family. This continued until they all ended up at the final family.

While Marcelino had been talking to Prairie Flower, Salvador had gotten up and was now coming out of the bedroom with the wooden wagon he had made, and a package inside the wagon contained Salvador's most prized memento. Salvador handed the wagon to Marcelino and told him it would also help him with his chore of bringing in the firewood. He took the package out of the wagon and handed it to Prairie Flower. Marcelino wanted to see what her present was and helped her take the wrapping off her package.

Prairie Flower saw the yellow dress, jumped up, hugged Salvador, and took off to her room. She put on the dress, and when she came back out, Salvador's mind was flooded with memories of his Angelita, but he thought that Angelita was smiling down upon them.

As Prairie Flower walked back into the living room, she said, "I will wear this dress tomorrow." She then gave Marcelino the little four-inch bottle that shimmered in many colors and placed around Salvador's neck a little wooden cross suspended by a thin strip of leather.

They sat for a little while longer before bidding one another good night and going to their bedrooms.

The sun shone bright that morning as the three inches of snow on the ground glistened.

Marcelino kept asking, "We need more firewood, Papa."

Though the box that contained the firewood was full, Salvador relented and said, "Maybe one wagon full of wood would do."

Marcelino put on his coat and handed Prairie Flower hers as he held her hand in one hand and the handle of the wagon in the other. At the door, she let him out first with the wagon and followed behind him.

Salvador looked out the kitchen window and saw Prairie Flower having Marcelino get in the wagon as she pulled him to the woodpile. He continued to watch as they filled the wagon about halfway when Marcelino made a snowball and threw it at her. Salvador laughed, watching them have a snowball fight for a little while.

They came back inside laughing, both covered in snow. After bringing in the firewood, they left the wagon outside by the door and sat down to eat breakfast. The last of the dishes had been put away, and in the distance, they could hear guitar music as everyone was coming.

They all stepped outside, standing there side by side, Prairie Flower in the center between Salvador and Marcelino. They stood there until the group finished singing "Las Mañanitas" and began to welcome everyone into the house.

Salvador gave each of the men a shot of whiskey as they continued to sing songs of old, talking and joking between songs. In the meantime, Prairie Flower was giving the women and children sweets and apple juice.

The celebration lasted about two hours. As each family left, Salvador handed each of them a large bag of apples and walnuts, for the crop had been large this year.

Chonita had noticed the dress that Prairie Flower was wearing, and when she was about to leave, she pulled Salvador to the side where others could not hear her and told him, "Mi corazón está alegre por ti" (My heart is happy for you). Then she got on the surrey and they departed.

Chapter 15

Return to the Arroyo

Spring came early that year, and Salvador had his garden planted by the last week of April, as had all the others. Plans were made to head out on the hunting trip on the first day of May.

Salvador had the covered wagon ready to go with War Bonnet tethered behind. They climbed aboard with Marcelino between them as they headed off to Gregorio's.

At Gregorio's, he and Marcelino climbed down as he thanked his brother for watching Marcelino. Gregorio asked if Prairie Flower was staying also, but Salvador told him no and explained how, in these last few months, the anger and hatred that had filled his heart had melted away. But now, he had to do the honorable thing.

"Lo siento, mi hermano" (I hurt for you, my brother), said Gregorio.

Salvador climbed back aboard, and as they headed off to join the others, they both looked back and saw Marcelino crying.

The others were waiting for him, and when they saw Prairie Flower, they did not say anything out of place. Instead, Antonio joked, "You forgot how to cook, but at least you hired one for the trip." They said farewell to their wives. As Chonita saw Prairie Flower, she began to cry, for in her heart, she knew her best friend was leaving.

"Tonight we will be in Las Vegas," Jose said as they headed off.

*****

They left Las Vegas, passed the mountain that resembled a wagon being pulled by oxen, and refilled their water barrels at Willow Springs. Going over the pass, most of the mountain peaks were still covered in snow. The days went by so fast for Salvador as they crossed the Purgatoire River and headed for the arroyo.

Arriving at the arroyo early in the day, the others noticed how Salvador had become more withdrawn and pensive day by day since they had crossed the Purgatoire River.

As they sat around the campfire that night, Antonio said, "We will need to kill a few more this year because we have the new family of Raphael and his wife, Antonia Solano, who are cousins of Antonio, three generations removed, and also the widow Feliz."

As they drank their coffee, Salvador said, "You know, Tomas, I think you were right. Did you notice how many more people were on the trail going either north or south? And it seems to me that the herd of buffalo we saw tonight is actually smaller."

Tomas said, "I told you that changes are coming fast, and I think this will probably be our last hunt."

It had taken three full days to make the necessary kills, and once they had finished making preparations to leave the next day, they went to bed exhausted.

Salvador got up at his usual time and saddled his horse and War Bonnet. Then he awoke Prairie Flower and asked her to wear her buckskin dress, which he had brought.

When Juan arose, he saw them riding down the arroyo and began to make breakfast.

They arrived at the end of the arroyo and dismounted. Standing there in front of their horses, they could see the campfires about three miles beyond the beaver dam. They stood there for a while, looking at the tepees and campfires of her tribe.

With the sound of the water splashing into the gorge, Salvador said, "There is your family." He knelt before her on one knee, bowed his head, and begged her forgiveness for having captured her.

Prairie Flower did not say anything, for she was drawn by the desire to see Little Pony and her father and mother again. She began to walk down the south side of the arroyo with the reins in her right hand. War Bonnet followed.

Salvador turned his back to her, for he could not bear to see her leave. As a tear of sadness flowed down his right cheek, he stood there in front of his horse, frozen in time for what seemed like an eternity. He took a step to mount his horse on the right side when, directly behind him, he heard, "Me voy contigo" (I go with you).

It was Prairie Flower's voice; and as his tears of sadness turned into tears of joy, he turned around, embraced Prairie Flower, and kissed her for the first time. Prairie Flower had replaced Angelita in his heart.

They saddled up and rode back to the camp. As they approached, the others were standing together, and they saw a giddy little boy with a grin from ear to ear ride in.

"El piojo y la pulga se van a casar" (The head louse and the flea are going to get married), Antonio said, referring to the bride and groom. "Now we will have to keep them separated until the wedding."

They climbed aboard the wagons and saddled up to head home.

The trip to the hunt had passed by so quickly for Salvador, and now the world was moving in slow motion, with each minute seeming like an hour. Finally, day one was behind them, and all that Salvador wanted was to get home as fast as possible.

*****

It seemed like a month had passed before they reached the first rancho, and now at least he could see himself getting closer to home as they passed each rancho and casa.

Finally, he pulled the wagon to a stop in front of Gregorio's as Marcelino came running to the wagon yelling, "Mamá, Mamá, mi mamásita" (Mother, Mother, my little mother). He went past Salvador to hug Prairie Flower. Gregorio was so happy for his brother because he had known that Prairie Flower had melted Salvador's heart before they had departed on the hunt.

The next day, Salvador left early in the morning to talk with Padre Sanchez. They talked for about two hours, making arrangements for the marriage, and it was agreed that Prairie Flower would have to be baptized before they could get married in the church.

Salvador went to Andre's home and asked if they would be Prairie Flower's godparents in baptism. They accepted immediately and wanted to know when it would occur.

"Tomorrow, Thursday, at ten," Salvador said. "I have already talked with the padre."

Next, he went to Antonio and Chonita's to ask if they would be the *padrino* and *madrina* (godfather and godmother) for the marriage. They accepted immediately because this was a very high honor. The godparents had responsibilities in the wedding and also in the marriage, participating in and contributing financially to the wedding details and providing guidance throughout the marriage. The *padrino* also gave the bride away.

Early Friday morning, the *padrino* and *madrina* came to pick up Prairie Flower. Though they already had a wedding dress for her, Prairie Flower wanted to get married in her buckskin dress that had fringe at the seams. They relented; and as was the custom, Prairie Flower would spend the night with them, as it was their duty to counsel her with marriage advice.

Early Saturday morning, Salvador and Marcelino left for Andres's to wait until it was time for the wedding. In the meantime, the friends of the bride and groom decorated their home with handmade wedding knickknacks. Paper doves and swans holding the couple's names, little straw note holders, and silver and gold cups were placed around their home.

Salvador was so nervous as he and Marcelino got into the surrey and began the trip to the chapel, both dressed in black suits with silver embroidery on each outside pant leg and on the cuffs of the jackets. The ruffles of the white shirts filled the entire front opening of the jackets.

Prairie Flower arrived at the chapel with Antonio and Chonita in her white buckskin dress and moccasins. On her head was a very tall comb from which draped a long white veil that covered her face and trailed three feet behind her. She was so beautiful, blending both the Spanish and Comanche cultures together.

Prairie Flower joined Salvador and Marcelino at the doorway of the chapel, for it was the custom that the couple would not enter the church for Mass until they were married.

The ceremony got underway, and after the padre blessed the thirteen gold coins, he handed them to Prairie Flower. The thirteen gold coins represented Christ and the twelve apostles. Prairie Flower then handed the coins to Salvador, who encased them in a handsome wooden chest and handed the chest to Antonio. Next, they exchanged vows. After that, Salvador took the coins out of the chest, showered the palms of Prairie Flower with them, and placed the chest on top of them. This gift of the coins and chest to his wife symbolized his complete trust and showed that his life was in her hands. Her acceptance was symbolic of her complete trust and her promise to care for him.

The ceremony continued with the tying together of the bride and groom. The padre took a large rosary and wrapped it around their wrists in a figure-eight, beginning with Salvador. Once tied together, they remained so for the remainder of the ceremony conducted in the chapel. The tying together symbolized the eternal unity and love the couple would share. Once the ceremony was complete, the padre removed the rosary and handed it to the couple as a memento of their commitment to each other.

Once they walked out of the chapel, the shouting, loud music, and gunfire started as everyone threw cornmeal into the air, which was believed to scare away and appease any evil spirits hovering around the newlyweds.

Later in the day, there was dancing. During the celebration, friends and family members offered best wishes and gave the couple gold coins. The first dance consisted of everyone forming a giant heart-shaped ring with the couple in the middle as they danced around them, singing and giving their blessing to the couple.

The sun had set long before they prepared to leave. Chonita kept Marcelino for the night as he had been tired out from all the activity of the day and was already asleep.

Arriving home in the dark, Salvador took care of the Arabian and put away the surrey while Prairie Flower, now in the house, couldn't help but wonder if she would be kicked out of bed tonight.

*****

The leaves of the cottonwood tree had already fallen when Prairie Flower went to assist Chonita as she gave birth to her first child. For two days, Chonita was in labor; and at noon on the second day, she named her firstborn Ambroso. Prairie Flower came home so happy and found Salvador in the meadow with the cattle, giving him the news that they would be Ambroso's godparents.

*****

The garden had already been planted when they were celebrating Ambroso turning one year old, and Prairie Flower began to have labor pains. Chonita immediately took over, and Prairie Flower gave birth to a boy the following morning at sunrise.

Salvador and Prairie Flower decided to name the baby Atilano and asked Tomas and his wife, Carmela, to be the godparents. Tomas and Carmela provided everything for the baptism, and the padre christened the baby Atilano Pumito. Tomas had added Pumito (Little Cougar) to his name.

*****

The years went by as fast as a day, and they lived each day as if it was their last, doing everything together. Each time friends came to visit, upon their arrival, Salvador would always quip, "Unda le ija ase coffee para que esta jente se vayan" (Hurry and make coffee so these people can get out of here), implying that they did not want anyone around because they were so in love. But that would just make the company stay that much longer, which was his intent, for they enjoyed company and all the joking and conversation.

*****

Three years had passed since Atilano had been born when Prairie Flower gave birth to a little girl, whom they named Conception Totsiyaa after Chonita.

*****

Time went by so fast as they made a living and raised their family that eight more years passed quickly. They found themselves in front of the chapel at Marcelino's wedding.

Marcelino and his bride, Maria, would come each Sunday to visit his parents. It was hard to believe that five years had passed as Marcelino's daughter, Maria Angelita, loved to sit and listen to the stories they would tell of Prairie Flower.

*****

A year had passed, and as always, the community would celebrate the harvest at the end of summer—a time to gather and have fun. This year, Tomas showed Salvador an article he had read about how the Comanche, a proud nation of over twenty thousand strong, had been devastated by smallpox, killing the elderly and the very young. Now they estimated that only about twelve thousand Comanche were alive. On that day, Prairie Flower mourned for her parents because Tomas had stated that Manuel Avila had sent word that Prairie Flower's parents had died during the smallpox outbreak.

That same year, as the leaves fell off the cottonwood trees, they found themselves again at the chapel doorway with Juan and his wife, Maria; for now it was Atilano and his bride, Floripa, who was Juan and Maria's daughter.

"How had the years gone by so fast?" Salvador wondered. For once spring arrived, his Conception would be marrying Enrique, the son of Don Pantaleon, who lived a day's ride away.

*****

Salvador and Prairie Flower looked forward to every Sunday, for now their family kept getting larger. Two years had passed, and Floripa had given birth to a baby girl named Maria Adelina; and Maria, Marcelino's wife, was with child again and was due in the fall.

*****

Time was going by so rapidly that it seemed that with each Sunday visit, there was another grandchild. Now, just ten years after Marcelino's wedding, it was early spring when Prairie Flower began to have small red spots on her tongue and in her mouth. The following day, the spots were on her chest, arms, and legs as she began to have a high fever. Salvador did everything he could to help break the fever and kept hoping that the red spots would blister, but they would not. He continually tried to make her as comfortable as possible, but on the third day, she came down with pneumonia. After two days of suffering, God took her.

Salvador had her buried in her yellow dress under the shade of the willow tree, on the left side. Almost every family in the community had lost a loved one to smallpox that year, and even Atilano had lost his wife, Floripa.

Chapter 16

Little Wooden Cross

Salvador would still be awake at the same time and go through the motion of taking care of the animals, tending to the garden, and pruning the apple trees without any driving force. And whenever any people would come to visit him, they would most often find him in his rocking chair under the weeping willow tree, between his two loves.

No matter what anyone did, they could not bring Salvador out of his depression, for he had lost his Angelita and now his Prairie Flower. He died at home of a broken heart eight months later to the day.

His coffin was lowered into the ground at the base of the willow tree, between his Angelita and Prairie Flower. Centered on his coffin was the little wooden cross with the thin strip of leather that Salvador had always worn around his neck.

Nvmv Tekwapv

Comanche Language

In this language, normally, the beginning of the word is stressed. Otherwise, you will find an accent on the stressed syllable, just like in Spanish.

Vowels that are doubled, like in *onaa*, are simply pronounced at length. Voiceless vowels are indicated by underlining. They are the same as the voiced vowel, but they are like whispers.

Below is the Comanche alphabet (A, B, E, H, L, K, M, N, O, P, R, S, T, V, U, W, Y, Z):

- a—*ah*, as in *wander*
- e—between *a* in gate and *e* in get
- I—*ee*, as in *flee*
- o—similar to *o* in *hope*
- u—*oo*, as in *boot*
- v—*uh*, as in *lust*
- b—between *b* and *v* in English
- p—same as English but sometimes pronounced as *b*
- r—rolled, like Spanish *r*
- s—same as English
- t—*t* of *stop*, sometimes pronounced as an *r*
- w, y—same as English
- z—glottal stop, as in *uh-oh* (also used *aa* traditional question mark)

About the Author

The author of the fictitious and hilarious autobiographical story of his early childhood, *Boxcar Baby*, now brings you another fictitious story of romance and true love, embedded in what daily life must have been like many years ago, prior to the acceptance of Colorado and New Mexico territories becoming states.